L

Experimenting with Energy

Alan Ward

Illustrated by Zena Flax

T 16880   43536

CHELSEA JUNIORS
A division of Chelsea House Publishers
New York · Philadelphia

Contents

---

3 5 7 9 8 6 4

ISBN 0-7910-1510-6

Preface

"Energy is eternal delight," said the poet William Blake. You will find many moments of lively pleasure when you are doing the activities described in this book. Just doing everything for fun, then talking and thinking about what happens, will help you to get a better idea of what scientists mean by energy. Energy is the mysterious "go" of things, which makes them move and work. Although we can imagine, use and even sell energy, nobody actually knows what it is – not even the cleverest scientist!

For those of you wanting to think more deeply about the mystery of energy, I have put simple explanations, as clues to guide your understanding. This book will be valuable if my ideas will help you to ask clearer questions about energy. A wise person said that understanding questions is more important that just knowing a lot of facts.

Always take it for granted that everything you do might be risky – even very slightly so. Only the most obvious dangers can be thought of before they occur. Therefore, take my few warnings seriously, and do be sensible and take care over everything you do. Try not to offend other people when you are experimenting, and clear up any messes you make. Experimenting with energy is enjoyable, particularly so, because energy means motion – and anything that moves is apt to be exciting.

William Blake thought that energy was even more than the go of things. He thought that energy was the secret of a thrilling and startling way of being alive – and there is no way a scientist could disagree with that . . .

The "go" of things

Ask what energy is and the cleverest scientist will reply that nobody knows. It is a great mystery. But you could say that energy is the "go" of things – the go that makes them move, and works machines. When I was a child, my mother complained of my fidgeting; she said that I was always on the go.

Blow into a balloon until it bursts. I dare you to. Feel your lungs working. They are machines, squeezing breath, forcing it to go inside the rubber envelope. Air gets squashed into the balloon and the skin tightens, like stretched elastic, and hardens – until, after one more puff, "bang". The balloon explodes. Pieces of split rubber are shot everywhere – and it's even more fun if the balloon contains confetti!

You worked hard to inflate the balloon. Energy was stored in the springiness of squashed air and the tightness of rubber. When the balloon's breaking point was reached, the stored energy was transferred, all at once, making the explosion. A blast wave of air reached your eardrums and you sensed loud noise.

On a bitterly cold day, out of doors, inflate a balloon until it is "fit to bust". Use a party balloon pump. Guess what should happen if you were to bring the balloon into a well-warmed place, or if you were to float it in a sink of hot (not boiling) water. Then do one of these things.

Why a top stands up while it spins

By applying forces (pushes and pulls) to the handle of a metal toy top, you pump some "go" into it, making it turn faster and faster. Stop pumping and the top stands, spinning on its point like a ballet dancer. If the hollow top has holes in it, their edges catch the air, setting up weird vibrations which you sense as humming sound.

But forces of friction (or rubbing) with the air and the ground act like brakes, slowing the spinning, until the top begins to reel about like a drunken person – and is stopped. Its energy of motion is actually transferred to the air and ground as heat. (Rub your hands and they feel warmer.) Energy is also transferred to make sound waves.

It is energy that keeps the top standing while it spins. Drop small pieces of paper straight down on to its rotating surface, near the outer edge. Notice how these papers are shot away from the surface, along straight lines. The papers give you an idea of how atoms inside the top would fly away, if they were not connected to other atoms in the metal. Atoms in opposite parts of a spinning top are pulled sideways, with equal forces, in opposite directions. The result of these pulls (caused by energy of motion) is to keep the top standing.

the arrows represent equal forces acting on the top

Energy from outer space

Stir some earth and water in a wide pan to make a thick gooey mixture, and then throw a blob of mud into it. You have a model meteorite – a body speeding through space, that hits the earth. Observe the crater it makes. Damage done when the missile is forced to stop is proof that energy is transferred to the muddy mixture. Craters on the moon and the planet Mars were caused by rock-like meteorites. Every million years or so a meteorite measuring a half mile across strikes the earth – and transfers as much energy as would an explosion of all the world's nuclear bombs.

The impact of a super-meteorite would raise so much dust that the sky would darken for years – so scientists think. Without sunlight and warmth, the world freezes, plants stop growing and animals, including people, die. Without the sun, the world would be like an endless, pitch-black winter's night. Such a "winter" might have killed off the giant dinosaurs, millions of years ago.

The Energy Crisis

harnessing wind power

But even with solar energy (that is, energy from the sun), there is not enough energy for life in modern times. Most of the extra energy needed comes from coal and oil, substances that were formed over millions of years from ancient plants and microscopic animals. Eventually, the supplies of coal and oil will run out. This worry is called the Energy Crisis and is why we need to save energy by using fuels sparingly.

harnessing water power

So, whether or not there may one day be a world disaster with a super-meteorite (or nuclear bombs), we have to worry about future energy supplies. By the way, although there is one in a million chances of that meteorite arriving this year, it is unlikely to happen in your lifetime . . .

Make an exploder

Buy a roll of percussion caps – those used to make toy pistols go bang – and, with scissors, snip one cap off the roll. Break a marble-sized ball of putty into two equal pieces and mould them around *under* the heads of two "three-inch" (7.5cm) steel nails. Squeeze the toy cap between the nail-heads and at the same time use your fingertips to press the putty to form a seal around the nail-heads. Take care not to force the substance between the nails.

putty
moulded
around nailheads

percussion cap
between nailheads

Dangle the object by holding one of its nail points. Stand **safely** on a chair. Then let the device fall, say about 2 yards, to strike a paving stone or concrete surface. When the bottom nail is stopped suddenly by the hard ground, its energy of motion is transferred – to create pressure and generate heat between the nail-heads. So the cap should explode.

As well as hearing a bang, you may see a flash of fire when gases from the mini-explosion force a hole in the seal.

The further an object falls, the harder it is likely to hit the ground. (Falling off that chair would probably hurt more than if you just fell over.) Will the exploder work if it is dropped from less than an inch above the ground? Will 2 or 3 caps make a louder bang? Try dropping it from higher up – **but do everything safely**.

Potential and kinetic energy

Energy in action is shown by motion. It is called kinetic energy. The word "kinetic" means "moving" and is related to the word "cinema" – where you go to watch a movie. Examples of kinetic energy are waterfalls, sound waves, flapping wings and creeping crawlies.

 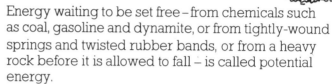 

Energy waiting to be set free – from chemicals such as coal, gasoline and dynamite, or from tightly-wound springs and twisted rubber bands, or from a heavy rock before it is allowed to fall – is called potential energy.

Potential energy is dormant, or "sleeping". The word "dormant" is related to the name "dormouse" for a creature that sleeps through the winter months.

Strike a light

Potential energy can be changed into useful kinetic energy. If you strike a match to observe the following ideas, **do it safely, out of doors**.

The energy that will make a match-stick burst into flame is hidden, dormant inside chemicals on the match-head. Scraping the match on the rough side of a match-box heats these chemicals – by friction – and they catch fire. Burning releases their potential energy, to produce greater heat, light, a cloud of gases and a slight sound of flaring. Observe the movement of the flickering flame and the swirling bluish smoke. You can imagine how fast the heated chemical atoms must be whizzing about – but they are too tiny to see individually.

Burning is an important way of converting potential energy into useful kinetic energy. Light from the match could be used to find a keyhole in the dark. Heat from the match could be used by a motorist to warm the car-key before trying to unlock a car-door lock that is jammed by ice.

Bangle booby-traps

Stretch a rubber band across the middle of a cheap plastic or metal fashion bangle (one that is not very thick). Insert a quarter between the middle parts of the band – and start winding up the rubber by twisting the coin. Put the object under a book. When somebody picks up the book, the "thing" jumps about. It is quite a surprise.

Improve the basic idea by taping the coin to the rubber, by using a tougher rubber band, or by taping paper flaps to each side of the coin. The tips of the flaps will hit the bangle and make more sound when the bangle booby-trap is sprung by an unsuspecting person (the "booby"). Have fun experimenting.

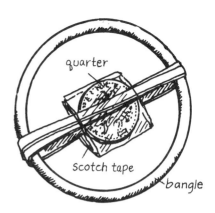

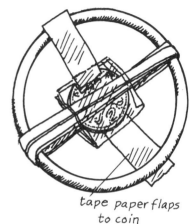

tape paper flaps to coin

Froggy pops up

Tape one end of a broken short, thin rubber band to the top front of one playing card and tape the other end of the band to the top back of a second card. When the cards are held together, with the band between them, insert a third card in the middle, forcing down the rubber. Hold the three cards in a bundle by gripping their bottom edges. Ease your finger pressure to make "froggy" jump out. (It's more fun with picture cards, with a picture frog in the middle . . .)

card1

card3

card2

front of card (card 1)

back of card (card2)

use picture card for card 3

These games are about potential energy becoming kinetic energy.

Tale of a tin frog

Prologue

As you may have guessed, energy comes in different forms. They are chemical, mechanical motion, radiant rays (like sunshine), thermal (making things hot), acoustical (producing sounds), electrical-magnetic, nuclear (released from the sun and from nuclear power-stations), and a puzzling form, sometimes called "positional". Positional energy is the potential energy to fall and do damage of a heavy mass that you have worked hard to raise – against the pull of gravity – into an "uphill" position.

Frog power

I have a solar-powered toy frog. It is worked by clockwork machinery using mechanical energy. So how can it be solar-powered (worked by the sun)?

Nuclear reactions inside the sun release nuclear energy which is transferred – across 93,000,000 miles of space – as forms of radiant energy, such as light and warmth.

Sunlight provides the energy for maize corn to grow. In the green leaves of the maize plants, solar energy is transferred to make substances, such as starch, that the plants need. These chemical substances are built up from materials which the plants get from the air and from the soil. The solar energy remains hidden as potential energy in the starch and the other chemicals.

While I am eating my breakfast corn flakes, I notice words printed on the box that say: "With Sunshine Energy in Every Flake" . . .

Machines which make electricity get their energy from burning coal and oil. The heat from the burning is transferred to make high-pressure steam. Energy from the steam is transferred to make magnets spin inside coils of wire. This causes electric currents to flow in the wire – and some of the electricity is used to operate machinery in factories that manufacture corn flakes from maize corn.

When I munch my corn flakes, juices inside my body act on the starch in them, converting it into sugar that can get into my bloodstream. *Sugar is the fuel that drives my body's machinery* – such as muscles in my arms, wrists and fingers – and blood carries the fuel to my muscles.

When I wind up the frog's clockwork, I transfer potential energy from sugar-fuel, to provide mechanical energy that for the time being is stored (as potential energy again) in a spring inside the frog's tin shell. Winding also wastes some energy – as the sound the winding makes, and as heat. I feel very slightly warmer.

At last I put down the frog. It hops away cheerfully – driven by mechanical energy now being transferred from the unwinding spring. Behold a solar-powered frog!

But I have not mentioned positional or uphill energy. The corn needed rain to fall from the sky. Heat energy from the sun put the rain up in the sky, when it made water from lakes, rivers and seas evaporate. Before the rain fell, it had uphill energy.

corn flake factory

take in energy

wind up frog

let it go!

Ballet of the grapes

After reading the thoughtful "Tale of a tin frog" you deserve to relax. Here are some exciting projects with water – but they will reveal more ideas about energy.

Tame submarine

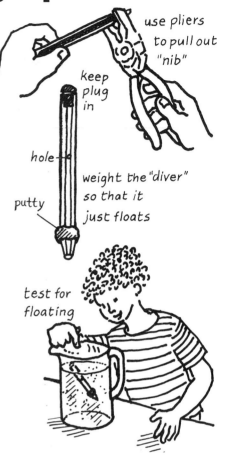

use pliers to pull out "nib"

keep plug in

hole

putty

weight the "diver" so that it just floats

test for floating

With pliers, pull out the "nib" and ink reservoir from a clear-sided ballpoint pen – but leave the little plug in the end of the tube. Mould putty around the other end, just above the opening, to make the tube slightly heavier. Keep testing it in a jug of water, *until it only just floats*. Float the tested pen-tube in a half-gallon clear plastic bottle that you have filled *to the brim* with water. Screw on the metal cap. You have a Cartesian Diver – named after a famous scientific philosopher. Notice the air bubble inside the top of the floating pen-tube.

Squeeze the middle of the bottle between both hands. Energy is transferred through the water, to provide enough force to squash the air inside the pen-tube into a smaller space. You make the bubble smaller – but the air inside it is denser (thicker) and springy. A small bubble is less buoyant than a larger bubble, and so your diver should sink.

Stop squeezing. This allows the "spring of the air" (which was storing energy inside the bubble) to force some water out of the tube. The bubble becomes buoyant enough again to make the diver rise. Watch the water-level in the tube changing as you operate this toy. Can you make the diver hover halfway up the bottle? (You feel your fingers changing their pressure slightly, all the time you are doing this trick.)

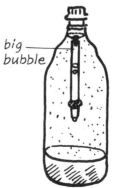

big bubble

small bubble

Bubble dancers

Put 4 or 5 grapes into a large glass of freshly-poured clear, fizzy lemonade. The grapes sink, but they are rapidly covered with gas bubbles, which lift them to the surface. There, as bubbles burst and more bubbles come out of the water, the grapes rock and roll – as buoyant bubbles act on them unevenly.

After some minutes, the grapes start to dance. At first, losing too many bubbles, they sink – only to attract more bubbles and rise again. And so the up-and-down ballet of the grapes continues.

Where does their energy come from? At the lemonade factory, carbon dioxide gas (which gives the lemonade its slightly acidic, refreshing flavor is forced under pressure into sugary water – mechanical energy from a pump is transferred to make the gas dissolve. When you open the bottle, pressure on the lemonade is reduced, so energy reappears to make the gas bubbles. (Thermal energy – warmth from the room – also helps the bubbles to form.)

Experiment to find out if you can get other slightly denser-than-water objects to dance. Try trouser buttons, mothballs (colored with wax crayons) and raisins.

Rubber band motoring

Squeezy bottle tractor

Cut off the stopper, and then remove the plug from the opening of a plastic washing-up liquid bottle. Use a big nail to force a hole in the middle bottom of the bottle. Knot together two rubber bands (mine were 0.2 in wide and 3 in long) and hitch one of them on to a paperclip, before feeding the bands through the hole you have made into the bottle. The clip stops all the rubber going in. Use a long hooked wire to "fish" through the top opening of the bottle and catch the bands. Pull them through.

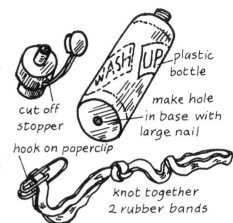

cut off stopper

plastic bottle

make hole in base with large nail

hook on paperclip

knot together 2 rubber bands

Hook one end of a shorter, 4 inch-long wire to the rubber. Pass the straight part of the wire through the bottle's perforated plug, then through a small bead, and wind the wire around the top end of a knitting-needle. Press and snap the plug back on the bottle. Now put some twist and tension into the rubber bands, by winding the knitting-needle, say 20 times. Put the tractor on the floor and watch it go – driven by its rubber band motor.

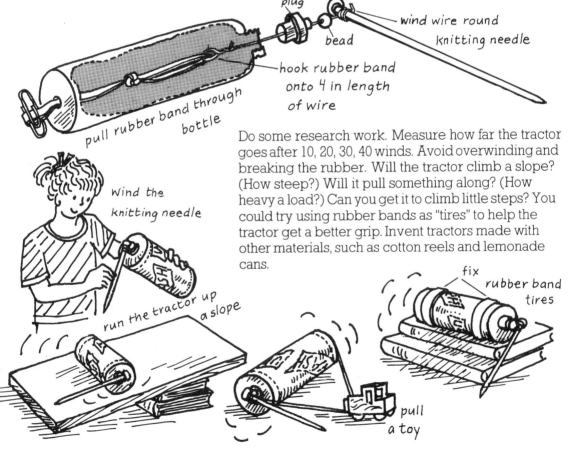

plug

bead

wind wire round knitting needle

hook rubber band onto 4 in length of wire

pull rubber band through bottle

Wind the knitting needle

run the tractor up a slope

Do some research work. Measure how far the tractor goes after 10, 20, 30, 40 winds. Avoid overwinding and breaking the rubber. Will the tractor climb a slope? (How steep?) Will it pull something along? (How heavy a load?) Can you get it to climb little steps? You could try using rubber bands as "tires" to help the tractor get a better grip. Invent tractors made with other materials, such as cotton reels and lemonade cans.

fix rubber band tires

pull a toy

Motorized geometry

Trace the pentagon. All its 5 sides and angles are equal. Then paste the tracing on to cardboard and cut out the shape, to make a template for drawing around. Use it to draw two identical 5-"petalled" flower patterns on stiff card. Cut out these patterns and carefully fold each one along the five straight lines connecting the pentagons – but do not press the folds too hard.

Use a rubber band to loop the two flower patterns together as shown. The rubber should not be stretched too tightly. Put this flat object under a book. Lift up the book – and you receive a pleasant surprise. The rubber contracts (shortens), acting as a motor – and transfers its energy to make the patterns spring up to make a solid-looking form called a dodecahedron. Have fun decorating it!

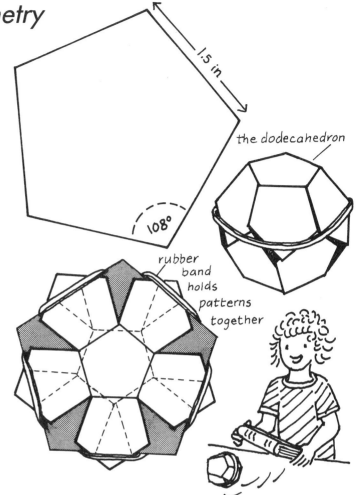

1.5 in

108°

the dodecahedron

rubber band holds patterns together

Indoor aerodrome

(The word "aerodrome" originally meant "airplane").

At many toy shops you can buy a model propeller-driven airplane complete with wheels, for a few dollars. You also need a thin, straight iron wire, about one yard long. You should obtain this at a model-maker's shop. Fix a blob of plasticine to one end of the wire. Poke the plasticine just inside a bottle half filled with sand. Bend over the wire and hitch a bent-back part of its far end under the assembled airplane's wing. Fix the wire there with tape. Set up this "aerodrome" in a room where there is plenty of space. Wind up the plane's rubber motor – and let the model take off, fly round the bottle a few times, and land. Enjoy yourself!

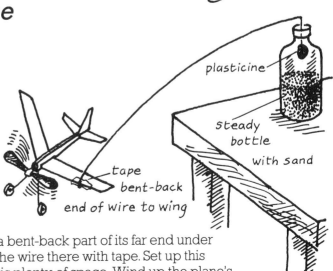

plasticine

steady bottle with sand

tape bent-back end of wire to wing

Molasses bomb – or poltergeist

When objects fall over without being pushed, people sometimes accuse a *poltergeist* – a German word that means a "noisy ghost".

Theory

The diagrams show a long polystyrene food tray (from a supermarket) balanced on top of a toy brick. Inside the tray at one end is a small mass – such as a die (wrongly called a "dice"). The tray is acting as a lever.

1 The lever balances.

2 If the mass is moved to the left, the lever is unbalanced, and so it tips and falls off the brick.

3 In this diagram the die has been replaced with a transparent hollow object, containing a mass concentrated on its right side. The lever balances.

4 If the mass could shift a little way to the left, it would be like moving the mass to the left in diagram 2 – and the lever would tip.

The situation in diagram 4 could happen if the mass inside the container was a fluid that would flow slowly down and to the left.

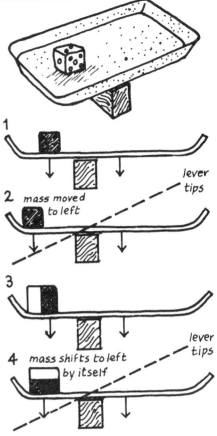

1

2 *mass moved to left*

lever tips

3

4 *mass shifts to left by itself*

lever tips

A spooky molasses bottle

Half fill a plastic pill bottle (mine is 3 in tall) with molasses. Stand up the bottle, with its cap screwed well on – and let the molasses settle for a minute or two. Afterwards, balance the bottle *on its side* on the brick, to project over the edge. Judge it so that the bottle just stays on the brick's edge. Watch the molasses flowing. The heavy mass shifts by itself – the bottle unbalances, and so it falls off the brick. You could call it a "poltergeist".

How the spooky molasses bottle works

molasses is invisible in a dark bottle

"priming" the bottle – letting the molasses settle to the bottom

molasses starts to flow but the bottle still balances

now the bottle falls

Transfer of positional energy

You burnt up a corn flake or two to lift up the fluid mass inside the bottle. You gave the molasses more potential uphill, or positional, energy. Some of this energy was used when it was transferred to provide kinetic energy (motion) needed to make the molasses flow sideways. And some of the energy made the flowing fluid very slightly warmer.

You can use the molasses bottle to trigger a safe, but noisy explosion.

The molasses bomb

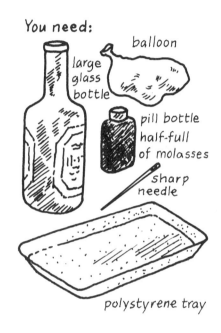

You need:

balloon

large glass bottle

pill bottle half-full of molasses

sharp needle

polystyrene tray

Tape a fully inflated balloon half way up on the side of a big glass bottle. Fix a sharp sewing needle in one end of a polystyrene tray, which you will balance on top of the bottle. Prime the small bottle "trigger" by letting it stand. Set up the lever, with the bottle – now resting on its side and pointing left – just behind the needle and over the balloon. Stand aside and wait. Count off the seconds. If you judge everything nicely, the lever tips, the needle pierces the balloon – and "bang" goes a molasses bomb!

Experiment to use the molasses bottle to switch on a light, or trigger an alarm.

Ben Boa – "Solar Serpent"

hang Ben Boa from ceiling with putty

Ben Boa

tray

hot water bottle

Copy Ben Boa on to thin card, add color and cut him out. Knot a piece of cotton, thread it through the hole between Ben's eyes, and fix the other end of the thread to the ceiling with putty. Wait until the twisted cotton unwinds itself – then Ben Boa should hang still. Ask permission to fill a hot-water bottle with hot (not boiling) tap water. Gently – so as not to disturb the air too much – hold the bottle flat, just under Ben. Watch the model rotate.

The serpent toy is driven by kinetic energy from rising hot air. If you hold a tea-tray between Ben and the bottle, Ben's gyrations slow down. Guess why.

When the model snake is hanging still in a very cold room, hold your bared arms beneath the coils. Thermal energy from your body heat warms the air – and the heated air rises. Watch Ben slowly come to life. Some of the energy you consumed with your breakfast corn flakes is transferred to do the work of driving the spiral machine (a duller name for Ben's body).

You know that corn flake energy is – by way of a chain of energy transfers – actually solar energy. To drive Ben by using solar energy directly, you need to make a 3-sided "black tower" with a door-like opening at the bottom. Fold, cut and paste a piece of rough-surfaced black paper, measuring about 16 x 24 in, like this:

fold black paper 16 × 24 in into 3-sided "tower"

cut out "door"

Where sunlight is streaming into a *draughtless* room, suspend Ben Boa. Wait until the spiral is still. Then stand the black tower just underneath, where the sun can heat the black surface. Black paper absorbs radiant energy from the sun, warming the air in and around the tube. Solar energy is transferred to cause a rising hot-air current that activates the snake-machine.

Purify water with a solar still

Shipwrecked sailors, and airmen who have to parachute from their damaged aircraft into the sea, can increase their chances of surviving by distilling drinkable water from dangerously salty sea-water. They use a special still which is included in their survival kits.

It works something like this:

Put some muddy water in a wide dish or pan – you could use a cardboard box lined with black plastic. Stand a small glass with a stone inside it, in the middle of the pan. Cover the whole apparatus with plastic wrap, but rest a small stone on the covering, to make a good dent above the glass. Now put this model solar still where the sun's radiation can reach it.

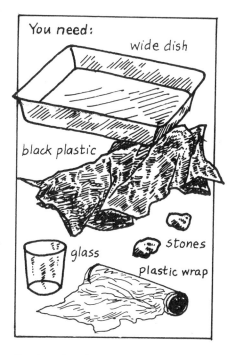

You need:
wide dish
black plastic
glass
stones
plastic wrap

- pour muddy water in dish
- stand glass (containing stone) in dish
- cover with plastic wrap
- rest small stone on plastic wrap above glass

line dish with black plastic

During the day, pure water evaporates, condenses on the plastic wrap and drips – as clear water – into the glass. The stone in the glass is to stop clear water evaporating again.

Now, **using very clean material, to be safe**, repeat the experiment, putting clean salty water in the pan instead of muddy water. Later taste the water that collects in the glass.

Working for fun

Energy is the "go" of things. However, this is only an easy way to say that energy can work things and do work. Without energy providing pushes and pulls to drive its machinery, a washing-machine is useless. It does not work – and you could also say: "It does no work". Even a simple machine like a screw-driver must be driven, by a human operator. When you use it to force in a screw, you burn sugar-fuel in your muscles, making them contract – to apply a pair of forces (through your fingers pushing and twisting opposite sides of the handle), to work the blade. Some people mention twisting, with pushing and pulling, as a third way to apply energy as force.

Sometimes a waterfall is called a "force". Its kinetic energy (mechanical motion) can be used to push around the blades of a special water-wheel, called a turbine, to generate electricity. This idea shows very nicely how energy and forces are connected. But, to a scientist, work is only being done when a force produces motion. The push of water trying to get out of a turned-off tap is not doing any work. But, when you squeezed the bottle containing your pen-tube Cartesian Diver, you did do some work, because you forced water to move up inside the tube, to squash the air bubble.

Try this demonstration of how a force can be transmitted (passed on) by levers. **Do this safely, with used matches**.

By pressing the first stick you can topple the match-box. Yes, you are doing work here, because your push makes things move.

The mousetrap bomb

A mousetrap is a nasty little machine which stores energy in a spring – but it is a clever machine. A kinder-than-normal use for a mousetrap is as a mechanical bomb. Explosive chemicals release their stores of potential energy when they explode. Your mousetrap bomb will release its energy after being detonated by way of a fuse. Detonator and fuse consist of wooden dominoes.

Form a long line of dominoes, standing them up, one behind the other. On top of the last one in the line, rest two more dominoes. Set the trap – **and mind you don't hurt your fingers** – before placing it with its trigger (where the cheese is supposed to go) just underneath the final "detonating dominoes". Rest two ping-pong balls on the metal snapper, to make the explosion more interesting.

Count down: 5 – 4 – 3 – 2 – 1 and "Fire" . . .

By standing up the dominoes you give each of them a little positional, uphill energy. Your push – no doubt fuelled by breakfast corn flakes – starts a chain reaction, setting free the energies of the dominoes, toppling the detonating dominoes and triggering the bomb. Then, "snap" goes the snapper, sending the balls flying.

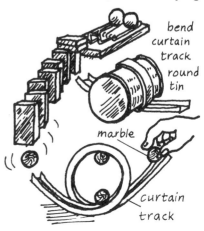

bend curtain track round tin

marble

curtain track

If you are ambitious, rig up a looping track for a marble by gently bending a metal curtain rail around a big tin, as shown in the picture. Can you get a marble to roll down the track, loop the loop, then whizz off the end, to knock over the first domino?

Waves transmit energy

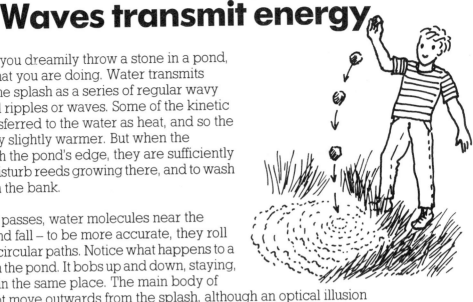

The next time you dreamily throw a stone in a pond, think about what you are doing. Water transmits energy from the splash as a series of regular wavy motions called ripples or waves. Some of the kinetic energy is transferred to the water as heat, and so the pond gets very slightly warmer. But when the wavelets reach the pond's edge, they are sufficiently energetic to disturb reeds growing there, and to wash away soil from the bank.

When a wave passes, water molecules near the surface rise and fall – to be more accurate, they roll around along circular paths. Notice what happens to a leaf floating on the pond. It bobs up and down, staying, more or less, in the same place. The main body of water does not move outwards from the splash, although an optical illusion makes it appear so. Your eyes are distracted to follow the motion – and your brain confuses your judgement.

direction of wave travel →

circular path of
water molecule

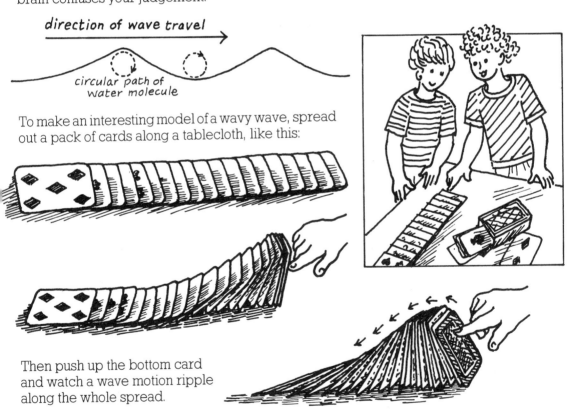

To make an interesting model of a wavy wave, spread out a pack of cards along a tablecloth, like this:

Then push up the bottom card and watch a wave motion ripple along the whole spread.

Radiant energy from the sun can get across what is apparently empty space. Unlike water waves, radiant energy waves can travel without having molecules of a substance to transmit them. It is impossible to imagine what radiant energy waves are really like.

"Intelligent" marbles

Rest a line of large, equal-sized glass marbles, to touch each other, on one end of a track made by connecting straight sections from a model railway.

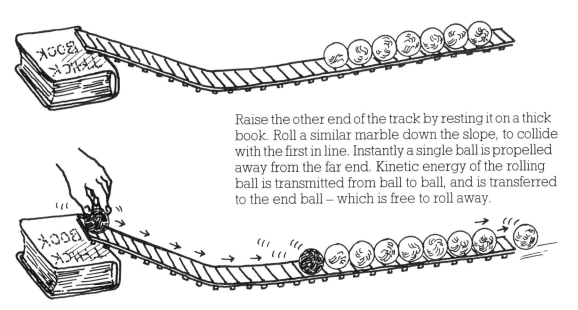

Raise the other end of the track by resting it on a thick book. Roll a similar marble down the slope, to collide with the first in line. Instantly a single ball is propelled away from the far end. Kinetic energy of the rolling ball is transmitted from ball to ball, and is transferred to the end ball – which is free to roll away.

The marbles are (believe it or not) elastic. When they collide they get slightly squashed and flattened. Then, when they return to their original shape, they pass on kinetic energy to the next ball – although some of the energy is also transferred as heat.

You have a model of a type of energy wave called a longitudinal wave, because, as it travels along, it vibrates lengthwise, unlike a wavy wave which vibrates up and down, or from side to side. Sound is transmitted by longitudinal waves. They depend upon the elasticity of air (or some other carrying substance), and so sound does not travel through empty spaces.

Can you get the marbles to "count", by rolling 2 or 3 balls off the end of the track? (You could pretend to your friends that you have trained the marbles.)

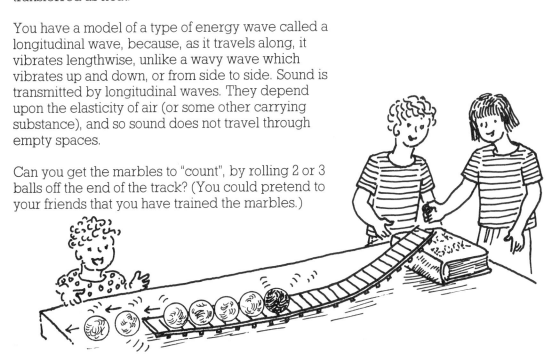

What goes up must come down

Before the modern Space Age, when a spacecraft launched from earth might be lost amongst the stars forever, it was true to say in ordinary life that, sooner or later, what goes up must come down. The old proverb put the idea of positional or uphill energy very nicely.

Younger children are mystified by a thin, round chocolate box or tin that rolls up a slight slope by itself. But, to you who understand about uphill energy, the explanation is obvious.

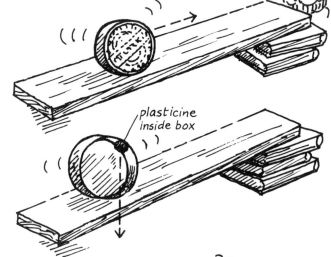

plasticine inside box

You stuck a heavy blob of plasticine on the curved part, inside the box. When you put the box on the bottom of the slope, you made certain that the plasticine mass was raised. You did a little work on the plasticine by lifting it up – against the pull of gravity – and gave it some uphill potential energy. When you let go of the box, the plasticine came down – giving the whole box kinetic energy to make it go up the slope.

Experiment with different boxes, slopes and masses. Find a way to stop a smooth box from skidding on the slope.

Following the picture, make a water-jet boat, to be driven by a "gravity motor" – using uphill energy. Kinetic energy to drive the boat is transferred from the uphill energy of the raised water. The water rushes out of the tube in a jet, making the boat move in the opposite direction, on a voyage in your bathtub.

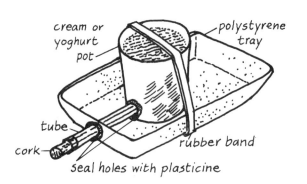

cream or yoghurt pot

polystyrene tray

tube

cork

rubber band

seal holes with plasticine

Make the vessel from a plastic cream pot, a polystyrene meat tray, a rubber band, a small cork, and a piece of tubing such as a ballpoint pen tube. Bore holes for the tube as well as you can, sealing any gaps with plasticine *before* getting anything wet. Start the engine by removing the stopper.

Magic railway

A Victorian engineer saw a trick with a couple of funnels, that fooled him into believing that he could make a railway carriage filled with passengers run up a mountain by itself (without expenditure of energy).

To see what he saw as a practical possibility, tape together the rims of two identical large plastic funnels, say, with 4 in diameters. Build a sloping track by resting two one-yard-long wooden rods between two books. One of the books should be about 1.5 in thicker than the other. The sticks should be touching at the bottom, but be spread apart at the top end of this sloping railway.

plastic funnels taped together

wooden rods each 2 yards long

THICK BOOK

BOOK

When you put the double-conical roller on the bottom of the track, it rolls up to the top – or so it seems *if you don't observe closely enough.*

Watch again, from the side this time, while you let the roller go. It actually *falls* as it travels along the track. What goes up must come down – the proverb explains all. (Think about it!)

Swingometer

A pendulum is a mass dangling from a string – like the ornamental pendant slung from a slim chain, looped about a person's neck. Gravity pulls this little mass, making it feel heavy – giving the mass its weight. Weight is the force you measure when you oppose the pull of gravity on things.

The string of a still pendulum is vertical (straight up or straight down). So a builder uses a pendulum to test a wall, to see if it is straight or leaning. The mass on the end of a pendulum is called a bob.

Investigate the number of swings, *from one side to the other* per minute, of a pendulum made from plasticine and thin string. The "string" should be measured from where it is tied, or from where you are holding it, to the middle of the bob.

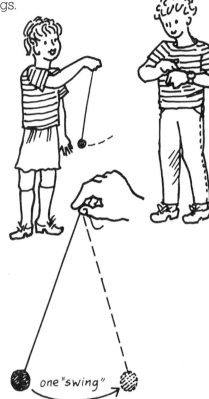

Mass	Length	Swings per minute
small plasticine ball (small marble size)	10 in 20 in 40 in	
large plasticine ball (large marble size)	10 in 20 in 40 in	

When you hold the string and lift up the bob you give the pendulum some uphill energy. Let go, and watch potential energy become kinetic – then potential again when the bob swings up at the other side – then kinetic, as the bob swings back – and so on. Can you observe the effect air resistance has on the pendulum?

Which of the variations you tested would make a convenient device for timing how many seconds your friends take to run around your houses, or the school playing-field? (Which pendulum takes one second to do one swing?) Use a "swingometer" to do timing tests.

"Hypnotized" potatoes

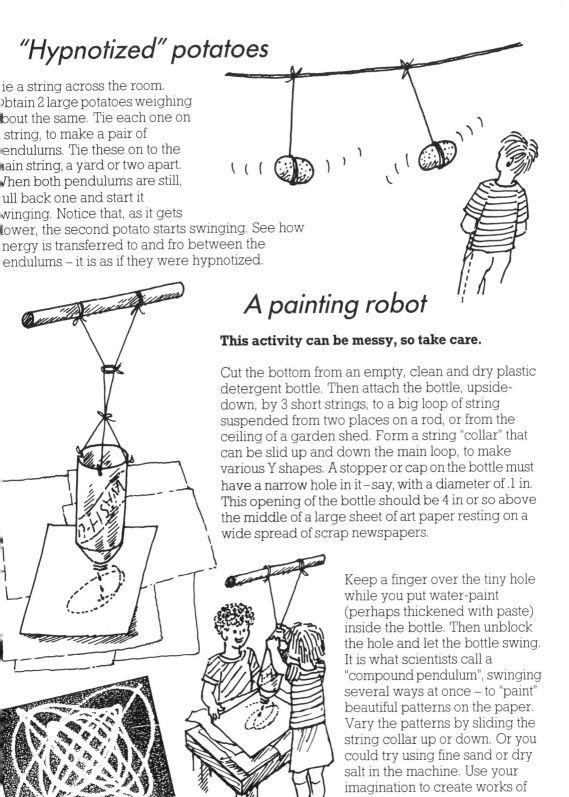

Tie a string across the room. Obtain 2 large potatoes weighing about the same. Tie each one on a string, to make a pair of pendulums. Tie these on to the main string, a yard or two apart. When both pendulums are still, pull back one and start it swinging. Notice that, as it gets slower, the second potato starts swinging. See how energy is transferred to and fro between the pendulums – it is as if they were hypnotized.

A painting robot

This activity can be messy, so take care.

Cut the bottom from an empty, clean and dry plastic detergent bottle. Then attach the bottle, upside-down, by 3 short strings, to a big loop of string suspended from two places on a rod, or from the ceiling of a garden shed. Form a string "collar" that can be slid up and down the main loop, to make various Y shapes. A stopper or cap on the bottle must have a narrow hole in it – say, with a diameter of .1 in. This opening of the bottle should be 4 in or so above the middle of a large sheet of art paper resting on a wide spread of scrap newspapers.

Keep a finger over the tiny hole while you put water-paint (perhaps thickened with paste) inside the bottle. Then unblock the hole and let the bottle swing. It is what scientists call a "compound pendulum", swinging several ways at once – to "paint" beautiful patterns on the paper. Vary the patterns by sliding the string collar up or down. Or you could try using fine sand or dry salt in the machine. Use your imagination to create works of art.

Little bangs

When a Party Popper is pointed up and away from other people, and the string attached to it is pulled, there is a little bang, a puff of smoke, a yellow flash and brightly colored streamers pop out, as from a cannon.

Kinetic energy to propel the streamers, to make the sound wave and to heat the flame, is released from potential energy stored in a mildly explosive charge of a chemical fulminate, or "detonating substance" – probably the same material used to bang toy pistol caps.

At the same fun party you may have noisemakers to pull. Look at one snap to see how it works. works. (Investigate a few from a cheap box of crackers – or save your party cracker, to take it apart.

Notice that a little of the fulminating substance is sandwiched and glued between overlapping ends of a pair of narrow cardboard strips. The strips are held tightly together by a small band of thin brown paper. This paper is gummed to the back of one of the strips. The other strip is not fixed, but is free to move sideways when a noisemaker is pulled. The little explosion happens when the gummed fulminate is broken apart.

Try making your own noisemakers, using toy caps as explosives. The main problem is to keep a cap still, while something rough – say, a fragment of fine glass paper – is scraped against it.

Party Popper

(take care)

cardboard strips inside noisemaker

fulminating substance

strips bound with brown paper

Only use Party Poppers with your parents' permission and while they are watching. **Do not take a Party Popper to pieces – this could be dangerous**.

Danger dust

This experiment needs to be done very safely, with adult help, out in the garden.

Obtain a fairly large metal canister of the sort that candies are sometimes sold in. You need a good-sized tin, with a not-too-tight-fitting lid – **not a press-in lid** and **not a screw-thread lid**. Ask an adult to help you bore a hole near the bottom of the tin, into which can be fitted one end of a plastic or rubber tube about one yard long. Stand a candle stub inside the tin.

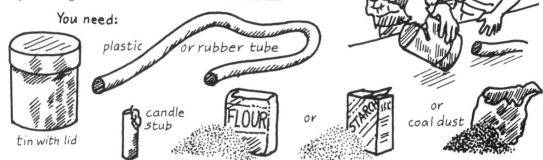

You need:

plastic or rubber tube

tin with lid

candle stub

FLOUR

or

STARCH

or coal dust

You also need very fine, dry inflammable dust. Try using flour or starch powder, or coal dust. The most suitable substance to use is Lycopodium, a powder made of millions of Lycopodium moss spores. (You can ask a science teacher.)

Put a *little* of the dust inside the free end of the tube. Light the candle in the tin. Replace the lid – *not tightly*. **Nobody must have any part of themselves over the top of the tin.** Blow into the tube – **but immediately take the end of the tube away from your face**, in case a "blow back" happens.

The blown dust should form a cloud inside the tin, catch fire suddenly and produce enough explosive force to blow off the lid of the can.

put some dust in end of tube

light candle and place in tin

blow into tube – remove from mouth **immediately!**

This innocent "bomb" illustrates how very fine inflammable dust, well mixed with air, sometimes catches fire inside an enclosed place, such as a factory or a coal-mine, to cause – in real life – a very dangerous explosion.

Transfer of energy as electricity

The professor was cleaning a dead frog's legs, when – much to his amazement – the legs gave a twitch. The year was 1780, the professor's name was Luigi Galvani, and he had touched the salty legs with two different metals. He realized that he had discovered a new source of electricity, which he decided to call "animal electricity".

In fact, he had discovered how to make a battery. Until that time the only way to make electricity was by rubbing things together, to make what today we call static electricity. When you rub a balloon on your pullover, you charge the balloon with so much static that you can get it to stick on the ceiling.

Another Italian professor named Alessandro Volta showed Galvani that animals were not essential to generate electricity – although a few animals, such as electric eels, do produce a powerful enough electric current to stun their prey before catching and eating it. You can make a simple Volta's cell, or battery, but first you need to make a galvanoscope (named after – guess who?), a detector of electric currents, to prove that your battery works. Wind up to 50 turns of thin insulated wire from an old electric bell around a toy compass. Leave about 12 in unwound at each end of the wire and bare the ends of these "leads". Tape the bared end of one lead to a copper nail, and tape the other end to a zinc-covered (galvanized) nail. You can obtain the nails from a hardware store.

You need:
thin insulated wire
toy compass
copper nail
zinc-covered nail
salty water or watered-down vinegar
lemon

Tape the galvanoscope to a table-top. The compass needle must be lined up with the wire windings. Dip the nails into a cup of salty water, or watered-down vinegar – or try a lemon that you have first rolled between your hands, to break its cells. Movement of the compass needle proves that chemical reactions are happening. *Energy is being transferred from the chemicals to make weak electric currents.* This is what happens when any kind of battery is operating. What happens when the nails are attached to opposite ends of the galvanoscope wiring?

Storing and releasing chemical energy

With this experiment you are making a model car battery – better described as an energy storage cell. **Only do this project with an adult, and be especially careful**. Lead is poisonous, so wash your hands afterwards. **Sulphuric acid damages skin, seriously hurts eyes, and spoils wood and fabrics.** If you are worried about using this, try a very strong solution of bicarbonate of soda in water instead.

Nail two 1 x 6 in strips of clean lead, one to each side of a stick that can rest across the top of a glass jam-jar. Nearly fill the jar with weak sulphuric acid – from an old car "battery". The separated strips of lead must dip into the acid.

Scrape the insulation away from the ends of two 16 in lengths of single-strand electrical wire, such as bell wire. Use a screwdriver to fix a wire to each connector on a bulb-holder – the sort of holder to take a 1.5-volt flashlight bulb. You also need the bulb. Tape the other ends of the wires to the lead plates of the cell. The light remains off. Your cell needs "charging".

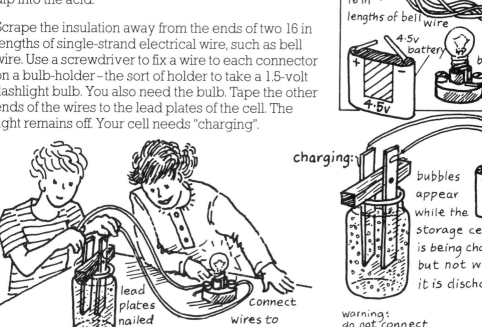

lead plates nailed to stick

Connect wires to bulb holder

Disconnect the wires from the cell. Then use two similar wires to connect the cell to the terminals of a 4.5-volt flashlight battery. (Don't try connecting the battery to the 1.5-volt bulb.) If the connections are satisfactory, gases fizz away from the lead plates in the acid – and one plate turns brownish. Current from the battery is causing these chemical reactions by supplying energy. Disconnect the battery after 5 minutes.

Then connect the leads from the bulb-holder to the storage cell. You will be thrilled to see the bulb light for a few seconds – proving that energy stored in the cell is being released and transferred to make electric current again.

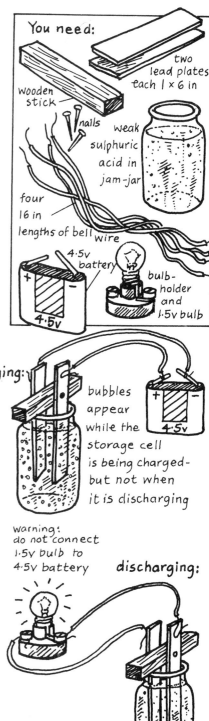

You need:

two lead plates each 1 x 6 in

wooden stick

nails   weak sulphuric acid in jam-jar

four 16 in lengths of bell wire

4.5v battery

bulb-holder and 1.5v bulb

charging: bubbles appear while the storage cell is being charged – but not when it is discharging

warning: do not connect 1.5v bulb to 4.5v battery

discharging:

How to see the "go" in a spin

Remember the experiment with the spinning top described on page 5. The next time you have a chance to see a pin wheel firework spinning, watch the ways the sparks are travelling just after they have been shot out from the coiled fire tube. They resemble what you noticed when energy from the top was transferred to the pieces of paper you dropped on the spinning surface. These ideas may remind you of what happens when energy from a spinning car wheel is transferred to moist mud!

In the middle of a **large spread** of newspaper, spin a saucer half-filled with watered ink, food coloring or water-color paint. You will obtain a pattern like the "fire-picture" made by a pin wheel.

enclose wet lettuce between two plastic colanders

attach one yard of string

You have noticed how sparks, mud and paint shoot away from spinning things. At first, they move away in straight lines, which start in the direction that the outer part of the spinner happens to be going in at the instant that the spark or mud, etc, is flung away. A mathematician would say that the lines are tangents to the spinning circles. A scientist would say that energy transferred to the materials gives them dynamic inertia – also called momentum. An engineer would say that he has a use for these effects in spin-drying machines.

Shut a wet lettuce between two plastic colanders. Tie the colanders together and attach one yard of string. Go outside and twirl around the colanders on the string. Mechanical energy transferred to the water makes the drops shoot away from this machine – leaving the lettuce much drier than it was before.

Kinetic art again

You need:
- electric motor
- battery
- paper-clips
- single strand wire
- nails
- rubber bands
- cork
- wooden board
- stiff cardboard
- corrugated card
- paper
- felt-tip pens
- paints

You need a 4.5-volt flashlight battery and a small electric motor, suitable for using with it. These motors can be bought at a model-maker's shop. Connect two single-strand wires to the motor and fasten a metal paperclip to the other end of each wire, for clipping the wires on to the battery terminal strips.

Using a tightly wound rubber band, fix the motor, pointing upwards, to a couple of nails that you have embedded in one end of a wooden strip about 14 in long. At the opposite end of the board, fix the battery, also using a rubber band.

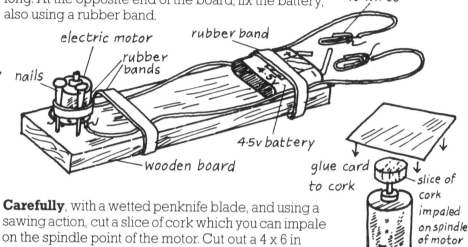

electric motor

rubber bands

nails

rubber band

wooden board

4.5v battery

attach paper-clips to wires

glue card to cork

slice of cork impaled on spindle of motor

Carefully, with a wetted penknife blade, and using a sawing action, cut a slice of cork which you can impale on the spindle point of the motor. Cut out a 4 x 6 in rectangle from thin but stiff cardboard and glue the middle of this card to the slice of cork. Don't be rough on the motor when attaching the cork and cardboard.

Stand the apparatus on a spread of newspapers. Surround the cardboard "turntable" with a "fence" made from a strip of supple cardboard – but cut a slot in the bottom edge of the fence, to allow the battery to be on the outside. Clip a paper square to the turntable.

surround turntable with "fence"

clip paper to turntable

Start the motor spinning. As the turntable spins, gently touch the paper with felt-tipped color sticks. You can create patterns of spirals and concentric circles. Better still, make thin pastes of poster paints and water and put blobs of these creamy colors on different parts of the papers, before switching on the machine. With practice and imagination, you can devise energetic art works. You could charge 10¢ per picture, to raise money at your next school fair. **But always be careful to avoid making a mess!**

An amazing "cling thing"

To make this entertaining machine, you need to wedge a yoghurt pot up through a circular hole which has been cut near one end of an upside-down polystyrene tray (mine measures 5 x 7 in). To make the hole, draw around an object, such as a small cup or jar, which is slightly less in diameter than the top of the yoghurt pot – then carefully cut the round opening. At the opposite end of the tray you need to erect a little post, a round stick such as a pencil. Bore a hole in the tray to take the post. Fix the bottom end of the post in a hole made in a slice of cork which is glued underneath the tray. (Cork can be neatly sliced with a sharp, wetted penknife, using a sawing action. **Don't cut yourself.**)

Make a small hole in the bottom of the yoghurt pot (now on "top" of the machine). Catch a rubber band on one end of a short stiff wire (4 or 5 in long). Then thread the other end of the band through a bead and down through the hole in the pot – before catching it on the middle of a cocktail stick, which will then be held in tension by the rubber, across the hidden opening of the inverted yoghurt pot. When you push the wire around, it winds up the rubber. When you let go, the wire is driven by the rubber-band motor.

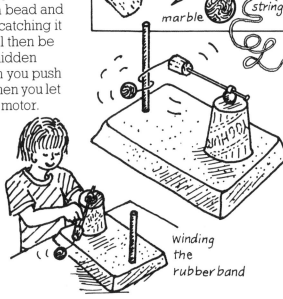

You need:
pencil or stick
yoghurt pot
polystyrene tray
slice of cork
bead
rubber band
4 or 5 in long stiff wire
cork
cocktail stick
marble
string

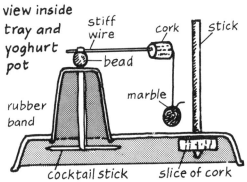

view inside tray and yoghurt pot

stiff wire
cork
stick
bead
marble
rubber band
cocktail stick
slice of cork

winding the rubber band

Attach a small cork to the end of the wire, before tying and taping on a light-weight object, such as a small marble. The object should dangle just above the tray. You will have to experiment, perhaps changing the position of the wire, while you are testing the amazing cling thing. When the wire rotates, the marble should swing out, causing its string to be caught against and wound around the post. This will stop the motor – while the marble has time to release itself. Then the wire will rotate again, and the interesting clinging and delaying action is repeated.

This kind of periodic delaying mechanism was once used to regulate clocks, to keep them running on time.

And an incredible "boomerang tin"

You are going to be reminded of the clown who went crazy while trying to throw away a boomerang. Here is a game with a large cylindrical tin that rolls right back to you, after you have sent it trundling across the level floor of a sizeable room – a school or village hall, without a carpet, being ideal. The activity shows how mechanical energy from muscular action can be transferred partly to do some work (moving the mass of the tin) and partly as potential stored energy, available to do similar work later on, but in reverse.

Use the largest tin you can obtain. Mine is a veteran of many successful demonstrations and it measures 6 in in diameter and 7 in long, but these measurements are not essential. You might ask a person in the catering trade for a tin that once contained coffee or cocoa. At each end of the tin (that includes the lid) bore two holes. Each hole should be 1 in from the center – so the two holes at each end are about 2 in apart.

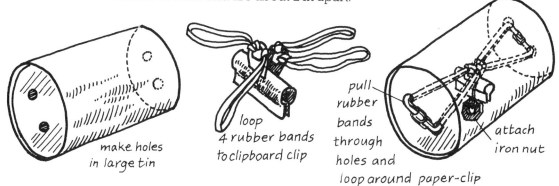

make holes
in large tin

loop
4 rubber bands
to clipboard clip

pull
rubber
bands
through
holes and
loop around paper-clip

attach
iron nut

Get a clipboard clip 2 in long and loop two rubber bands to each of its twin, holed upper parts. With the clip inside the tin, thread both pairs of rubber bands out through the ends of the tin (one of which is the lid) and fix the two bands at each end together, using a paperclip. Attach a heavy mass of some metal, such as iron, to the clipboard clip, before shutting the lid. Now for a test run: roll the machine across the floor. When it stops, snap your fingers – and it should (perhaps after minor adjustments) roll back obediently. Energy stored in the twisted rubber provides the driving force for the boomerang effect.

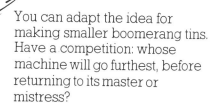

You can adapt the idea for making smaller boomerang tins. Have a competition: whose machine will go furthest, before returning to its master or mistress?

May poles and rampant reels

One of my favorite science action toys is a wooden model woodpecker, attached by a short spring to a bead that can just slide down a tall metal rod. When the bird is slid to the top of the rod, the gravitational pull on its mass causes enough friction between the rod and the bead, to stop the bead from slipping.

But when you touch the bird, to make it start vibrating up and down on its spring, the bead begins to slide down in little jerky movements – its descent being regulated by the vibrations. Positional energy is transferred in roughly equal amounts at regularly measured intervals. The bird, moving down with a life-like pecking action, takes perhaps 30 seconds to reach the bottom of the rod – where it could be used to trigger off one of those domino fuses, to detonate a mousetrap bomb (see page 21).

You can easily make a version of this toy by mounting a long wooden dowel rod to stand upright in a hole bored in a heavy block of wood. Make the spiral by winding a few coils of galvanized iron wire around a rod, such as a pencil, just thicker than the dowel rod. Bend the wire sideways at 90° at one end of the coil, to make a "tail", say, 4 in long. Impale a small plasticine ball on the tail. Now it is possible to make this "may pole" perform like the woodpecker – and perhaps you will like to disguise it as a bird, using feathers and a cocktail stick.

Does the small ball always take about the same time to get down? Can you use this idea to invent a timer? Experiment by changing the mass of the plasticine or the length of the tail. You could fix a small bell to the ball, to sound a cheerful jingle – and don't forget that idea about the exploding mousetrap!

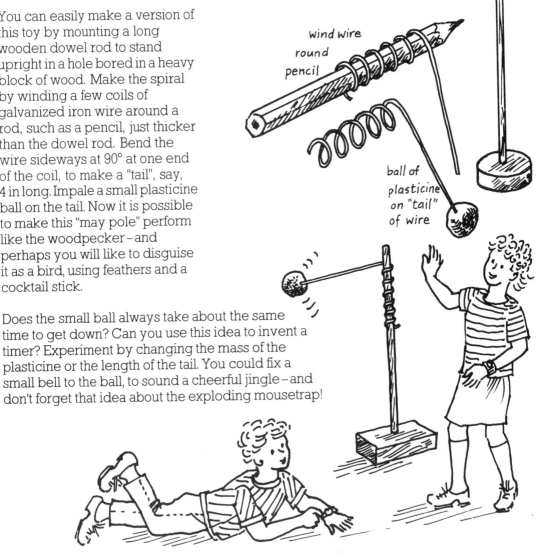

Wind wire round pencil

ball of plasticine on "tail" of wire

Scientific fun with "rampant" reels

cotton
reel

card
raised
on brick

Improvise a ramp. Prop up one end of a piece of thick board, using a ¾ in-thick toy brick, or Lego bricks. Put the slope at one end of a level floor that is covered with a carpet which does not have a deep, soft pile. Rule a "starting line" at the top of the ramp. Assemble several cotton reels, all of the same type.

By lifting a cotton reel to the starting line, you give it some positional potential energy. After you release the roller, it goes down the slope before running a little way along the carpet. There it is stopped by the braking forces of friction – with the carpet fibers and with air resistance. Assuming they do not collide with each other, do 3 cotton reels rolled down the slope, from the same height, all travel the same distance over the carpet – approximately?

Another way of asking this question is to say: are all the cotton reels capable of doing the same amount of work after leaving the bottom of the slope? A scientist measures work (which is another name for energy) according to how far a mass (a cotton reel) is moved (along the flat carpet). Repeat these tests with the same ramp raised 1.5 in then 2.5 in then 3 in high. Do the cotton reels roll further by roughly equally greater distances? Invent some variations on these tests.

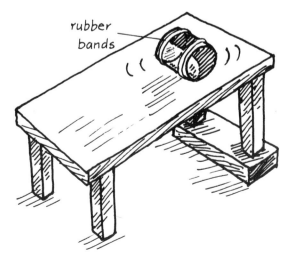

rubber
bands

The molasses machine

Put a pair of wide rubber bands (as "tires") tightly around opposite ends of a sealed glass jar that is half filled with molasses. Rest this roller at the top of a slope formed by propping up one end of a table – say a height of 6 in. Watch and marvel as this "molasses machine" descends at a snail's pace.

Measuring energy metrically

You are standing under an apple tree, when a nice rosy apple falls at your feet. Take a break. You can eat the apple. As you pick up the fruit, feel the force of its weight – the pull of gravity on it. Raise it to your lips, but – before taking a bite – stop!

Lifting the apple means doing work against the pull of gravity. This requires energy. *How much energy*? If the "go" of things is so essential to keep nature (including you) alive and working, how is it measured? It is impossible to talk sensibly about quantities and money values of energy, unless energy can be calculated.

a mass of 100g such as this apple weighs one newton

one joule of work is done when the apple is lifted up one meter

Say the apple has a mass of 100 grams (g), and you lift it straight up – through a vertical distance – a height of one meter (m). The force needed to lift a mass of 100 g is called a newton (N). *One hundred grams of mass weigh one newton*. The newton is also the scientific unit for any other force, whether a pull or a push.

Sir Isaac Newton 1642-1717   *James Prescott Joule 1818-1889*

The joule – a basic unit of work or energy

Motion is always a sign of energy. Work is done only when something is moved. *Work and energy are, in fact, the same*. The amount of work or energy needed to lift a mass of 100 g through a vertical distance of 1 m is called a joule (J) – also known as a newton-meter. One joule of energy is needed to push or pull with a force of one newton through any distance of one meter.

You used one joule of energy to pick up that apple. Now you can go ahead and eat it.

While you are munching you can start to think about how much you weigh – in newtons. Kilograms only tell you about your mass – the "stuff" made from atoms and molecules that makes up your body. Newtons tell you how much *force* of gravity acts on your body's mass.

How much do you weigh?

Say you have a mass of 60 kilograms. "Kilo" means a thousand, therefore your mass in grams is 60,000 g. To find out how much that weighs in newtons, break it down into 100 g lots. Divide 60,000 by 100. *Answer: 600 N.*

Now what is your real weight? Measure your *mass* in kg by dividing your weight in pounds by 2.21. Convert it into grams, divide by 100, and you have your weight in newtons.

How much energy do you need to go upstairs?

How many newton-meters or joules of work (energy) are needed to lift a 60-kg person up stairs that are 3 meters high? A 60 kg person weighs 600 N. To find out how much energy is needed, multiply newtons by meters. *Answer: 1,800 J.*

How many joules of energy do *you* need to go upstairs?

Energy values

Food and fuel can be made to transfer their energy, by burning – although biological "burning" is far less violent than burning coal and oil. The energy can be used to drive machines, such as cars and your body's machinery of muscles and bones. Heating values of foods and fuels can be given in joules, but so many joules are available that bigger energy units are necessary: kilojoules (thousands) and megajoules (millions). A kilogram of bread can supply 10 megajoules (10 MJ) of energy – that is 10,000,000 J, or ten million joules. A crumb of bread, weighing 0.2 g, can supply 2,000 joules (2 KJ) which is more than enough to take that imaginary 60-kg person up a 3-meter stairway. Apples can supply 2 MJ per kg. Gasoline contains 47 potential MJ per kg – imagine those 47,000,000 joules going up in a flash of orange fire!

Are you a human horse?

People often confuse energy with power. Energy tells us about the quantity of work. Power tells us how quickly the work gets done. A more powerful machine does the same work more quickly. If two cars that weigh the same race up the same hill, they do the same amount of work, going from start to finish, but the car that wins develops more power – *it does the same work in less time.*

The unit of power is the watt. It is one joule of work done in one second. If you took one second to lift the one-newton weight of that 100-g apple through a height of one meter your rate of working was one joule-second, or one watt (1 W).

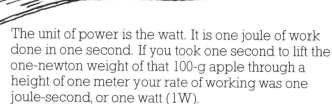

the "average horse"

Many years ago engineers began to compare the powers of machines with the power of an "average horse". Their power unit was the horsepower (HP), which is today equal to 750 W.

How to measure the power of your leg muscles

Begin by finding out how many joules of work you need to climb some stairs (multiply your weight in newtons by the height in meters. Borrow a stopwatch from a sports teacher. Get a friend to time you climbing the stairs as fast as you can. Then divide joules by the time in seconds, to find the power developed by your leg muscles, in watts.

I have just tested myself. My mass is 85 kg. I weigh 850 N. The stairs were 2.5 m high. I took about 2.5 seconds to run up the stairs. Much to my surprise, I discovered that – for my short burst of speed – I developed 850 W. This is greater than 1 HP. Now who amongst your friends is most powerful at running up stairs?

Be careful not to overdo these tests. Stop if you tire very quickly. And be careful on those stairs.

Making work easier – using energy more effectively

Ask an adult to help you find a rock (or other heavy object) that would be impossible for you to shift by yourself. Let the adult push one end of a long, strong pole under the rock. Then you have a go at pulling up on the other end of the pole. Perhaps you can shift the rock now. You will have to pull the pole up a long way, for the rock to move a short way – but the previously impossible task now gets done, by you.

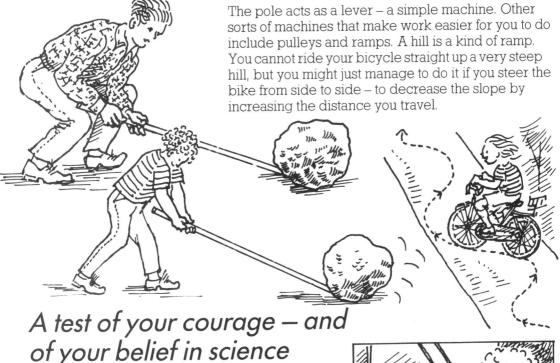

The pole acts as a lever – a simple machine. Other sorts of machines that make work easier for you to do include pulleys and ramps. A hill is a kind of ramp. You cannot ride your bicycle straight up a very steep hill, but you might just manage to do it if you steer the bike from side to side – to decrease the slope by increasing the distance you travel.

A test of your courage – and of your belief in science

Machines never apply as much energy usefully as we have to use to make them work – they are never entirely efficient. This includes your body machines. You have felt how some of the energy you put into hard physical work is wasted as heat. Try this daring test.

tin filled with sand

let go!

it swings back

Fill a tin with sand. Hang the tin from a string, in the middle of a doorway. Pull back the tin and hold it against your nose. Then (**without pushing it**) let this "pendulum machine" swing away – *but keep your nose very still*. When the pendulum returns, it stops in front of your nose. It does not hurt you! Some of its energy is wasted by overcoming air resistance. The machine's mechanical inefficiency guaranteed that your courage was not foolhardy.

Keeping heat in – or out

Out of doors, on a dry, cold, but not freezing night, stand for a short time in your bare feet, with one on a piece of fluffy carpet and the other on a stone path. It is a good idea to put the carpet outdoors for some time, before doing the test – **and don't allow yourself to be chilled**.

Notice how your feet feel. Which foot feels the warmer? Yes, the one on the carpet. Stone is a better heat-carrier, or conductor, than the carpet, so your foot on the stone loses its body heat more quickly. The carpet is a good insulator of heat – thermal energy passes through it more slowly. You could say that heat insulators stop heat energy from escaping too fast, although they can never keep heat in forever.

You must understand that the warmth you feel while standing on the carpet comes from your body. Expanded polystyrene is also a good insulator. It feels warm to your touch, but this is because polystyrene is not very good at taking away heat from your sensitive fingers.

Paper Jack

Tramps know a trick with newspapers to keep them from freezing to death in bitterly cold weather. A famous tramp called Paper Jack was well-known for this life-saving trick. He stuffed layers of newspaper underneath his clothes. The layers of paper trapped air. Newspaper and trapped air are both good heat insulators. So are straw, and the cloth rags used to insulate water-pipes to stop the water inside from turning to ice and splitting the pipes.

On a winter day you can prove to yourself how Paper Jack kept warm. A neat test is to stuff one wellington boot with newspaper, keeping the other boot free.

Haybox cookery

Scouts and guides use insulation to save energy by burning less fuel for cooking – they sometimes use a haybox. After bringing to the boil their porridge or stew, they put the lid on their cooking pot and place the pot inside an airtight wooden box lined with polystyrene, packing it all around, under and above, with straw. When the box is shut, heat gets out so slowly that the food goes on cooking.

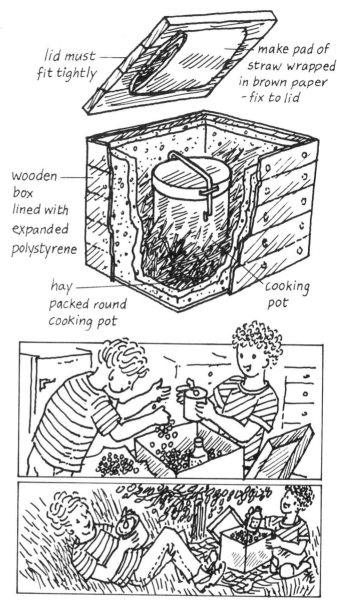

lid must fit tightly

make pad of straw wrapped in brown paper – fix to lid

wooden box lined with expanded polystyrene

hay packed round cooking pot

cooking pot

Cool drinks in the country

Expanded polystyrene, formed into nodules, is often used for packing delicate objects before sending them through the post. Collect a boxful of these nodules – aim to fill a large grocery box that has a lid. Small bottles or cans of ice-cold drinks, from your refrigerator, may be kept cool inside this box – for picnics in the country. This is because heat insulators are just as useful for keeping heat energy from getting in. Put the box in the trunk of your car.

bag of ice in tin

cardboard box

crumpled newspaper

How to keep ice

Test different ways of keeping an ice cube from melting for as long as possible. Starting with equal-size ice cubes, you could organize a competition with your friends. Try wrapping the cubes in newspaper, kitchen aluminum foil, polystyrene nodules – even in a blanket. Some children put a plastic bag filled with ice cubes inside a tin, before putting the tin inside a big cardboard box, and packing the tin – around, under and above – with crumpled newspaper. Some of the ice was unmelted after 12 hours in a slightly warm room. Can you do better?

The energy that money can buy

If your car goes 50 miles on a gallon of gas and gas costs $2 a gallon, it is easy to have a rough idea of how much energy you are obtaining for your money – enough to take you and your heavy vehicle to a place half a hundred miles away.

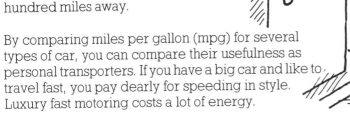

By comparing miles per gallon (mpg) for several types of car, you can compare their usefulness as personal transporters. If you have a big car and like to travel fast, you pay dearly for speeding in style. Luxury fast motoring costs a lot of energy.

Gasoline is made from oil, so as the world's oil in the ground gets less, gasoline will become ever more expensive. Until a cheaper fuel is available, it makes sense for motorists to prefer small cars with high mpg – they will save energy while saving money.

Paying for electrical energy

Electricity is also derived from oil. Potential energy from chemicals in oil is transferred as heat, through burning (see page 11), to move electric current which is supplied to our homes.

Ask your parents to show you an electricity bill. It will show how many units of electricity your family has used in a one month period. I have just been looking at one of mine for 1985. It tells me that I have to pay for 200 units at 12¢ per unit. One unit is also called a kilowatt hour – a unit of power.

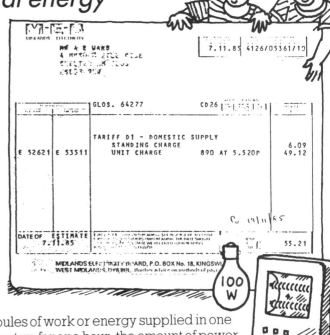

A kilowatt is 1,000 W, or a thousand joules of work or energy supplied in one second. If this rate of doing work is kept up for one hour, the amount of power supplied is one kilowatt hour (1kWh). With this 12¢ unit of energy I can keep a 100 W light bulb burning for 10 hours, or a 2,000 W (2kW) space heater going for half an hour.

How to read an electricity meter

How much electricity does your family use in a day? And how much money does it cost? To find the answers you need to know how to read an electricity meter. Ask your parents to show the meter to you.

It contains an electric motor, worked by a very small sample of all the electricity used in your home. The more current used, the bigger the sample and the faster the little motor spins. It drives a mechanism of gears and wheels that turn pointers around dials on the display panel. Only read the figures on the five big dials. From left to right, they stand for tens of thousands, thousands, hundreds, tens and units.

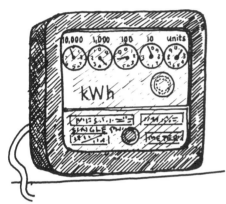

To read a dial you have to observe which way its pointer turns. For mechanical reasons, the pointers go alternately clockwise and counter-clockwise. You write down the figure on a dial that the pointer has just passed. The meter shown in the picture reads: 95,712 kWh units. To find out how many units are used at home in a day, begin by writing down today's meter reading, at a certain time. Read the meter again 24 hours later. Then subtract the first reading from the second:

Saturday	0900 hrs	7 899 kWh units
Sunday	0900 hrs	7 927 kWh units

$$
\begin{array}{r}
7\ 927\ - \\
7\ 899 \\
\hline
\end{array}
$$

Units used in a day	28

If a unit costs 12¢, these 28 units will cost $3.36

Note You may have one of the new meters with a direct digital readout, in which case reading the meter is easy.

Discuss with your parents how you might reduce the family energy bill.

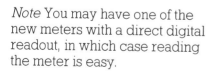

It's wise to be "energy-minded"

Be on the look-out for toys that use energy in unusual ways, such as the electronic clock which operates on "potato power". If you find this difficult to believe, make a dozen Volta's cells (page 30) by putting pairs of copper- and zinc-coated (galvanized) nails in small potatoes. Using short wires, and making good taped contacts, join the copper on one cell with the zinc on another. Then connect the spare copper and zinc potato cell "poles" with a bulb-holder containing a 1.5 V or a 1.25 V flashlight bulb. With patient effort, you should get the bulb to light. Electronic calculators and digital clocks can be run on very low rates of electric current – such as can be obtained from potato, banana, apple and Coca Cola "cells".

the "two-banana" clock

In toyshop windows, you may have noticed feathery toy birds bouncing up and down on long springs. If you own one of these, you can try using it as a timer. (Are there always the same number of bounces per minute?) You may have wondered why the shop window bouncers keep going all day – because, as you know, machines give back less energy than you put into their use. Remember the pendulum machine. So what keeps the display birds bouncing forever?

An interesting type of toy car is called "friction drive". You can charge it with energy by rubbing its wheels on the floor. When you put the charged car down, it runs for some distance. If you can afford to break open one of these cars – **and do ask an adult for help, if you think you could hurt yourself** – you will find that the energy you give the car is stored in the kinetics (motion) of a heavy spinning wheel, called a flywheel. It drives the car when you put it down. Engineers dream of inventing a pollution-free bus, driven by a huge flywheel. The wheel would be spun electrically overnight. The bus would run silently, and be slightly re-charged by brief electrical contact, at town bus-stops.

What you can do about the Energy Crisis

[H]omes, industry and transport [d]epend on energy from oil, gas [a]nd coal – but the world's [s]upplies of these fuels will [p]robably be used up within a [h]undred years. Thoughtful [p]eople are worried about the [c]oming Energy Crisis. Other [s]ources of energy, such as winds, [w]aves, waterfalls, direct solar [e]nergy, and heat from deep [d]own in the earth, may not be [e]nough to replace oil, gas and [c]oal. Nuclear power might solve [t]he problem, but it produces [w]astes that could poison our [p]lanet Earth. Scientists are [u]rgently busy, trying to invent [n]ew ways of producing immense [q]uantities of energy safely. You [c]an help by teaching yourself [e]nergy-saving habits:

Learn to be a safe cyclist and depend on body power

Dress warmly instead of turning up the room heating

Turn off lights and electrical machines after using them

Get used to walking instead of always going by car or bus

Keep the refrigerator door closed as much as possible

come in!

Don't stand chatting with the front door open

Energy savers

[A] market gardener became worried about the high cost of heating his green-[h]ouses. He solved his problem by keeping 500 rabbits in hutches amongst [h]is plants. Heat from the rabbits' bodies kept the plants warm – without electric [h]eating – and he sold the rabbits for their fur and meat.

How much is the yearly heating bill at your school? Do [y]ou think you could organize a "Switch it Off Year" (or [t]erm) to save energy? Your team will have to be strict [a]nd will have to stop draughts and close doors. *But [h]ow much money will you save?*

Index